Chloe,

Love from

....

I love you dearly,

Chloe,

and I love to watch you grow.

Each day you bring me far more joy
than you could ever know.

Chloe,

I love your sleepy eyes,
in the early start of day.

Your face is who I want to see
so we can run and play.

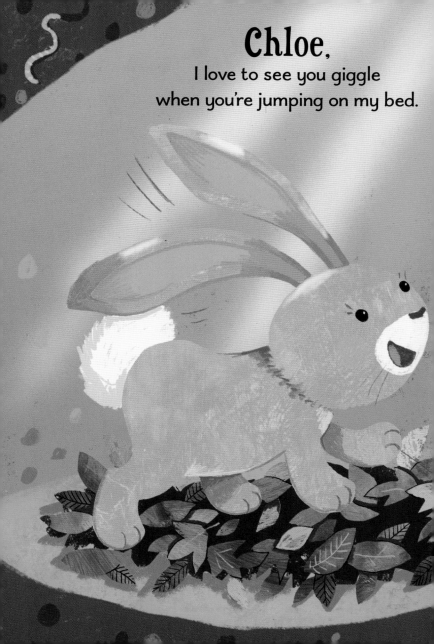

Chloe,
I love to see you giggle
when you're jumping on my bed.

To see your little dimples
as you laugh at what I've said.

Chloe,

I love the little noises that
you make each time you eat.

Taking tiny nibbles,
on a yummy, tasty treat.

Chloe,
I love your curiosity
as you discover and explore.

Watching your mind blossom,
into something so much more.

Chloe,
I love it when you're kind,
you're so thoughtful and so smart.

Working together with your friends,
you have such a caring heart.

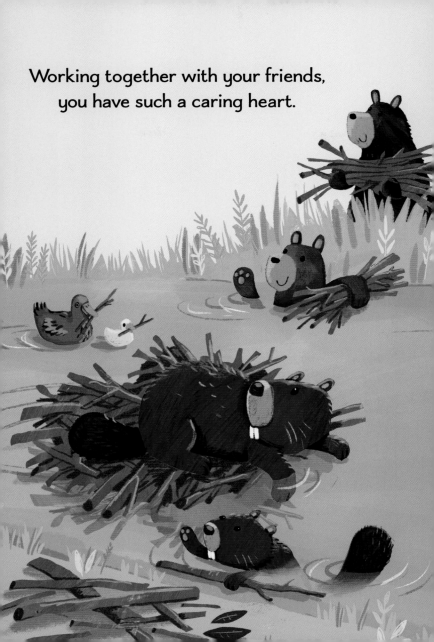

Chloe,
I love those little games you create, learn, and play.

I'm your biggest fan,
I'll forever feel this way.

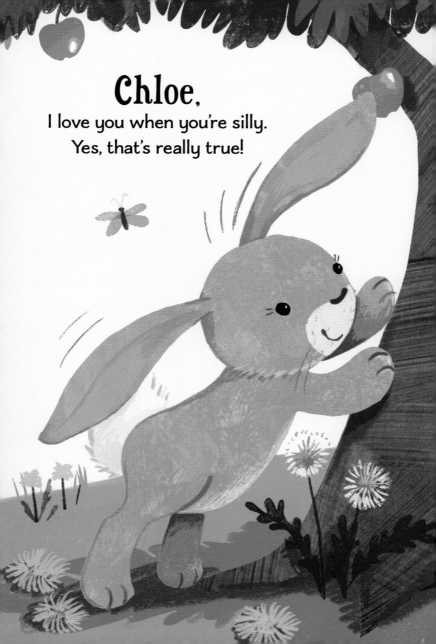

Chloe,
I love you when you're silly.
Yes, that's really true!

You are so very funny
in everything you do.

Chloe,
I love that look of joy when
you get bubbles in your hair.

Even when you're splashing
lots of water everywhere!

Chloe,

I love it when you share,
your stories and your dreams.

Spending time together,
counting stars and moonbeams.

Chloe,
I love your little sleepy face
when you begin to yawn.

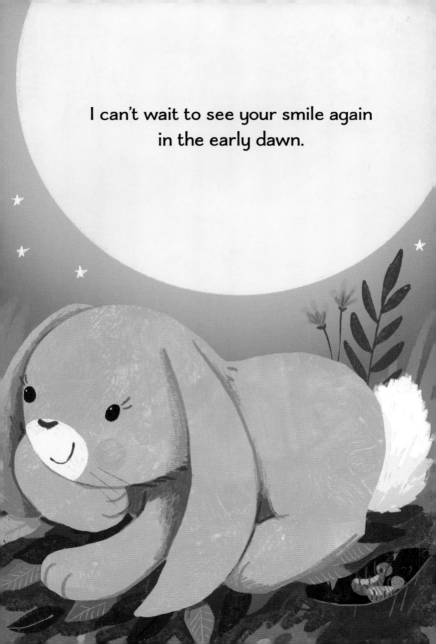

I can't wait to see your smile again
in the early dawn.

Chloe,

I love everything you say
and all the things you do.

But most of all I love you
just for being YOU!

All the things
I love about
Chloe

Chloe,
draw a picture of the things that you love!

Written by J.D. Green
Illustrated by Joanne Partis
Designed by Ryan Dunn

Copyright © Orangutan Books Ltd. 2020

Put Me In The Story is a
registered trademark of Sourcebooks, Inc.
All rights reserved.

Published by Put Me In The Story,
a publication of Sourcebooks, Inc.
P.O. Box 4410, Naperville, Illinois 60567-4410
(630) 536-1104
www.putmeinthestory.com

Date of Production: October 2020
Run Number: 5019356
Printed and bound in Italy (LG)
10 9 8 7 6 5 4 3 2 1

MIX
Paper from
responsible sources
FSC® C023419

put me
in the story®
Bestselling books starring your child!
www.putmeinthestory.com